W9-BDH-362

THE WACKY SUBSTITUTE

By Sally Derby

Illustrated by Jennifer Herbert

Marshall Cavendish
New York London Singapore

Text copyright © 2005 by Sally Derby

Illustrations copyright © 2005 by Jennifer Herbert

Marshall Cavendish, 99 White Plains Road, Tarrytown, NY 10591

www.marshallcavendish.us

Library of Congress Cataloging-in-Publication Data

Derby, Sally.

The wacky substitute/ by Sally Derby ; illustrated by Jennifer Herbert.—1st ed.

p. cm.

Summary: When Mr. Wuerst, the substitute kindergarten teacher at Merryville School, drops

his glasses into the frying pan one morning, he ends up wearing a dish towel to school instead

of his scarf and he mistakes the class gerbils for fur caps.

ISBN 0-7614-5219-2

[1. Substitute teachers—Fiction. 2. Schools—Fiction. 3. Humorous stories.] I. Herbert, Jennifer,

ill. II. Title.

PZ7.D44174Wac 2005

[E]—dc21

2004019452

The text of this book is set in Avenir.

The illustrations are rendered in gouache paint on Arches cold press 140 lb. paper.

Book design by Michael Nelson

Printed in China

First edition

1 2 4 6 5 3

One morning,
Mr. Wuerst's glasses
slipped off his nose
and fell into the frying pan.

The lenses shattered.

"My glasses!" cried Mr. Wuerst.

"What will I do now?"

Just then the phone rang. Mr. Wuerst picked up a banana and held it to his ear. The phone kept ringing. Realizing his mistake, he dropped the banana and fumbled for the receiver. "Hiram Wuerst, teacher, speaking," he said.

"Mr. Wuerst? This is Benjamin Carter, principal of Merryvale School. Our kindergarten teacher is sick. We'd like you to substitute today."

Ring

9

In spite of his broken glasses, Mr. Wuerst agreed to teach. But he couldn't see very well.

"Here, puppy, I have to leave," he said to his cat, giving her a bone.

"Be a good kitty," he told his puppy. He threw the puppy a catnip mouse.

Then, mistaking a dish towel for his scarf, he wrapped it around his neck and started off for Merryvale School.
Along the way, he tipped his hat politely to several snowmen.

When Mr. Wuerst got to school, he walked down the hall, trying to read the names on the doors. "This looks right," he told himself, opening the door to the custodian's closet.

"Mr. Carter, good to see you again!" he said to a mop.

Fortunately, Miss Duggleby was passing by at that moment.

"You want Mr. Carter?" she asked. "Right this way."

"Excuse me," Mr. Wuerst told the mop. "I hope I didn't disturb your class."

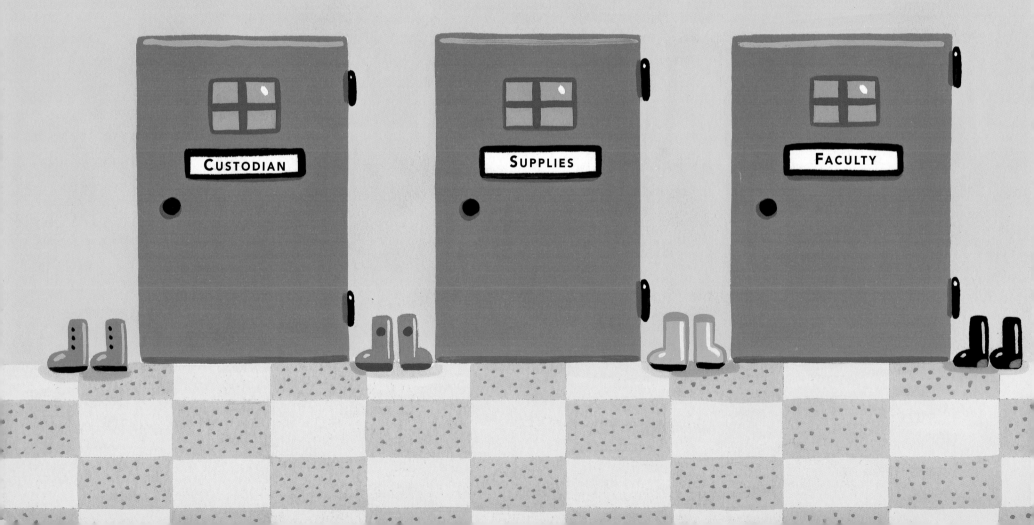

In the kindergarten room, the boys and girls were already hanging up their coats and hats and scarves. Mr. Wuerst hung up his coat and dish towel.

A cushion on Ms. Darling's chair looked like the attendance book, so he picked it up and held it close to his nose.

"Hmm, I can't read this without my glasses," he told the class. "We'll just skip attendance. Let me introduce myself. I'm Mr. Wuerst. It's spelled W-u-e-r-s-t and pronounced *worst*. I'm really the best, though, so you can call me Mr. Best, if you like." This was an old joke of Mr. Wuerst's, but it was new to the kindergartners. They burst into giggles.

Mr. Wuerst walked over to the gerbil cage. "What a lot of fur caps," he said. "Haven't seen one of these since I was a boy." He opened the cage and reached in. Twelve gerbils jumped out. While the boys and girls chased the gerbils over tables and under desks, Mr. Wuerst worried about story time. How would he be able to read? He would just skip the story, he decided.

At ten o'clock Mr. Wuerst announced, "Time for snacks."

"Not yet!" shouted the boys and girls. "Story time comes first."

"Ah, yes," said Mr. Wuerst. "Who would like to read today?"

"You read. We listen," the children told him. Mr. Wuerst picked up a book from Ms. Darling's desk. He looked at the picture on the cover. "Oh, good, it's *The Three Pigs*. I won't need my glasses for that," he thought

"Once upon a time," he began, "three little pigs decided to go out into the world to seek their fortunes."

"Not pigs, puppies!" cried the boys and girls. "You're reading the wrong story!"

"Is that so?" said Mr. Wuerst. "Well, what happens to them?"

The children told Mr. Wuerst what happened in the story, while he kept turning the pages and nodding his head and saying, "I see," although he really couldn't, of course.

Snack time came. Mr. Wuerst opened the refrigerator and started handing out containers.

"Oh, no," the children protested. "That's Ms. Darling's yogurt."

"You don't say! Well, why don't you get snacks yourselves?" Mr. Wuerst suggested.

So, although Tuesday was "milk day," some children took orange juice and some took milk, and that made everyone happy.

At rest time, Mr. Wuerst pulled down the window shades. The kindergartners put their heads on their desks. Mr. Wuerst put his head on his desk, too. He was so tired from trying to see all morning, he fell asleep. He began to snore.

One after another, the kindergartners lifted their heads to see what the noise was. When they realized Mr. Wuerst was asleep, they tiptoed around the room, getting out blocks and crayons and clay and toy cars and paint. And the gerbils! They had a lovely time.

But it couldn't last, of course. At twelve o'clock the bell rang, and Mr. Wuerst woke up with a start. "What's that? Is it my alarm clock?" he cried.

"It's time for us to go," the children explained.

"Good-bye, then," said Mr. Wuerst. "You have been a fine class."

"That's not how we do it. You have to line us up and take us out to the bus," said the children.

"Is that right? Well, follow me."

Mr. Wuerst led the class through the halls and out the door.

The wrong door. He led them right to a hook and ladder truck.
"Here we are! All aboard!" said Mr. Wuerst.
With whoops and hollers, the children climbed up on the truck.

They swung from the ladders and blew the horn and rang the bell. The firemen came running. "What a shame. I thought I was seeing my first red school bus," Mr. Wuerst said, when the firemen pointed out his mistake and led everyone back to the waiting bus.

"Come back again, Mr. Wuerst," the children called. "You're the best substitute we've ever had."

"Thank you kindly," said Mr. Wuerst. He shook hands with the bus driver. "Mr. Carter, great school you have here. Fine boys and girls."

The bus driver gave Mr. Wuerst a funny look and shook her head.

Back in the kindergarten room, Mr. Wuerst put on his coat and wrapped his dish towel around his neck. He started down the hall. "Good-bye, all. I'm off to the eye doctor's," he said. And he opened the door to the girls' bathroom.

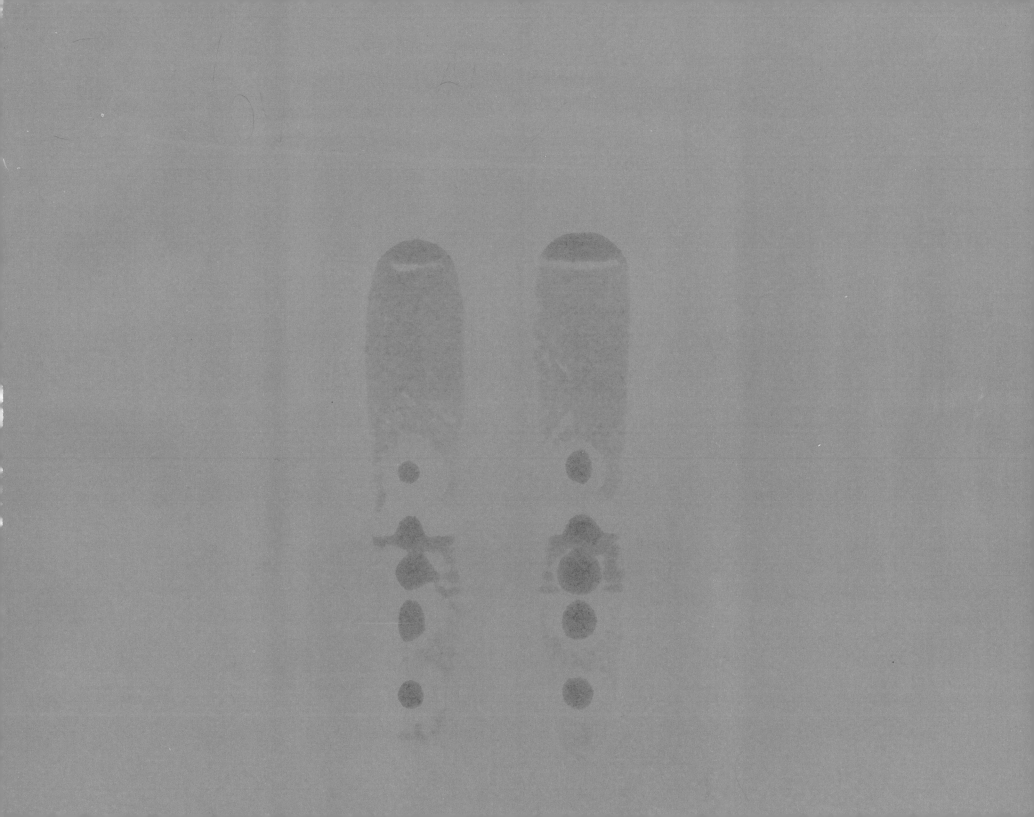

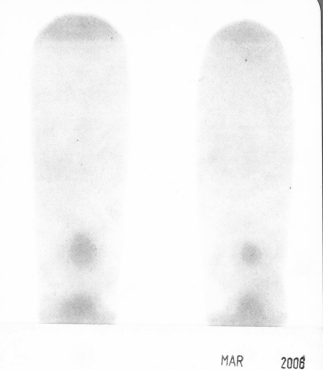